Can Cam win at the Dime Toss?

Eric gently tossed the coin. It slid past three circles and stopped just at the edge of the cardboard.

"We didn't win," Donna said.

Cam reached into her pocket. She took out a dime and said, "Let me try."

Cam sat on the ground. She carefully tossed the dime up in the air so that it landed flat on the cardboard. It landed near one of the circles.

"I don't see how anyone can win this game," Cam said as she got up from the ground. "It's just about impossible to get a dime right inside a circle."

"Let's try something else," Donna said. "Maybe we can win a prize at another booth."

THE CAM JANSEN ADVENTURE SERIES

CAM JANSEN
and the
Mystery of the
Carnival Prize

★ ★

DAVID A. ADLER
Illustrated by Susanna Natti

★ ★

PUFFIN BOOKS

To Eddie,
My best little boy

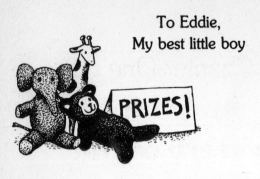

PUFFIN BOOKS
Published by the Penguin Group
Penguin Putnam Books for Young Readers,
345 Hudson Street, New York, New York 10014, U.S.A.
Penguin Books Ltd, 27 Wrights Lane, London W8 5TZ, England
Penguin Books Australia Ltd, Ringwood, Victoria, Australia
Penguin Books Canada Ltd, 10 Alcorn Avenue, Toronto, Ontario, Canada M4V 3B2
Penguin Books (N.Z.) Ltd, 182-190 Wairau Road, Auckland 10, New Zealand

Penguin Books Ltd, Registered Offices: Harmondsworth, Middlesex, England

First published in the United States of America by Viking Penguin Inc., 1984
Published in Puffin Books, 1992
Reissued 1999

5 7 9 10 8 6 4

THE LIBRARY OF CONGRESS HAS CATALOGED THE PREVIOUS PUFFIN BOOKS EDITION UNDER
CATALOG CARD NUMBER: 91-67506

This edition ISBN 0-14-130307-7

Printed in the United States of America

RL: 2.6

Chapter One

Honk! *Honk!*

The street was being repaired. Cars were lined up in both directions waiting to pass.

Cam Jansen squeezed the handbrakes of her bicycle. The bike stopped, and Cam got off. She waited for her friend Eric Shelton and Eric's twin sisters, Donna and Diane.

Honk!

"Why are people honking?" Eric asked as he got off his bicycle. "They know they have to wait."

Cam, Eric, Donna, and Diane walked with their bicycles past mounds of dirt and rocks and a large truck mixing cement. They walked past the long line of waiting cars.

"Hey," a woman called from her car. "Does one of you children want to trade your bicycle for my car?"

"I'm sorry," Cam answered. "But we're too young to drive."

As the children continued to walk, Diane asked Eric, "Does she really want to trade? We could give the car to Mom."

"She was just joking. If she was riding a bicycle like we are, she wouldn't be stuck in this traffic jam."

Cam and Eric were going to school to help with the fifth-grade carnival. It was spring vacation, and their grade was raising money to buy books for the school library. Donna and Diane were going to play the carnival games.

Cam, Eric, and the twins waited at the corner for the traffic light to turn green.

"I want to play the Ring Toss," Diane said.

"Well, I'm only playing games that have big furry stuffed animals as prizes," Donna said. "I plan to win one."

Cam said, *"Click,"* and closed her eyes.

Cam always says *"Click"* when she wants to remember something. "It's the sound a camera makes," Cam often explains. "And my mind is a mental camera."

Cam has what adults call a "photographic memory." They mean that Cam can remember every detail in an entire scene. It's as if she had a photograph of everything she has seen stored in her brain.

"There are fourteen games at the carnival," Cam said with her eyes still closed. "The only ones with stuffed animals as prizes are the Button Jar Guess, the Dime Toss, and the Baseball Throw."

Cam's real name is Jennifer. When she was a baby, people called her "Red" because she has red hair. But when they found out about her amazing memory and heard her say *"Click,"* they began calling her "The Camera." Soon "The Camera" was shortened to "Cam."

Eric pulled on Cam's sleeve and said,

4

"Let's go. The light has changed."

Cam opened her eyes. She walked with her bicycle across the street. Then the four children got on their bicycles and rode to school. They were stopped at the gate.

"You can't go in yet," the teacher standing by the gate told Cam. "The carnival hasn't opened yet."

"We're working in the carnival," Cam told the teacher. "My name is Jennifer Jansen. This is Eric Shelton, and these are Eric's sisters, Donna and Diane."

The teacher was about to check his list when he saw a tall boy with curly blond hair at the gate.

"Stop," the teacher told the boy. "You can't go in yet."

"I'm not going in. I'm leaving," the boy said as he walked past.

"Oh," the teacher said. Then he looked at his list and told Cam, Eric, and the twins that they could go in.

"That boy was probably helping," Eric said as they walked through the gate. "He was carrying a large roll of tape."

Cam, Eric, and the twins locked their bicycles in the rack near the schoolyard gate. Then Cam and Eric looked for their teacher, Ms. Benson.

6

"There she is," Cam said. "The rest of the class is already there. The meeting has already started."

"Remember, the children are coming here to have a good time," Ms. Benson said as Cam and Eric sat on the ground. "Now, those of you with booths, go and check that everything is in order."

Many of the children got up and walked to their booths. "You're my assistants," Ms. Benson told Cam, Eric, and the other children still sitting. "I want you to walk around and see that everything is in order. There may be lost children. Some booths might need change. And I want all of you to keep your eyes on the bicycles. Last year, one was stolen."

Ms. Benson looked at her watch. She clapped her hands and said, "It's ten o'clock. Let's open the gates. It's time for the carnival to begin."

Chapter Two

"Let's check the bicycle rack," Cam said to Eric.

"No. I have to find Donna and Diane. My mother told me to look out for them."

The schoolyard was already crowded. There were groups of children waiting in lines at the Button Jar Guess and at the Water Gun Shoot.

"Try your luck here. Win a great prize!" the girl at the Boat Race called out.

"Test your knowledge," the girl at the Trivia booth said.

"Great prizes here. Easy to win!" the boy at the Beanbag Toss shouted.

Eric stood on one of the schoolyard benches. He looked at the children standing near the many booths. Then he looked down at Cam and told her, "I don't see them."

"Maybe they're with the bicycles."

Cam and Eric walked to the bicycle racks. There was a long line of bicycles, all locked up. They found Donna's and Diane's bicycles. But the two girls weren't there.

"Look," Cam said and pointed to a red-and-blue bicycle. "This one isn't locked. That's probably what happened last year. Someone didn't lock his bicycle and it was stolen."

"I have to find Donna and Diane."

"I'll help you look," Cam told Eric. "I just want to take a picture of this bicycle. I want to remember what it looks like in case it's missing later."

Cam looked straight at the bicycle. She said, *"Click,"* and blinked her eyes. Then she told Eric, "I have a picture of the bicycle stored in my brain. Now we can look for the twins."

Cam and Eric walked past a few girls at the Water Gun Shoot. They were shooting water guns and trying to put out the flame on a candle a few feet away. A boy at the

Boat Race was blowing through a straw at a toy sailboat. He was trying to send it across a large tub of water.

"I see my sisters," Eric said. "They're at the refreshment stand."

Donna and Diane were waiting in line behind an older girl. The girl had long brown hair, and braces on her teeth.

"I'll take a cup of cola," the girl said.

The boy behind the counter pointed to a sign above him and said, "We have orange juice, apple juice, and milk."

"Yuck," the girl said. "Health food. All right, give me some of those whole-wheat pretzels and orange juice."

The boy gave her a bag of pretzels and a cup of juice. The girl paid him and began to walk away. Then she stopped and said, "Let me see the coins I paid you."

The boy held out his hand.

"I need this one," she said, and took one coin back. "It's my lucky dime." She gave the boy another dime and walked away.

"I'll have some orange juice," Donna said.

"And I'll have apple juice," Diane told the boy.

Cam and Eric waited while the two girls drank the juice. Then Eric said, "I thought you planned to win a stuffed animal. Why aren't you at one of the game booths?"

"I don't know which one to try," Donna said.

Bong! Bong!

The boy at the Dime Toss booth was

hitting the bottom of a large metal pot with a wooden spoon. "We have a winner! We have a winner!" he shouted.

"Look," Eric said. "It's the girl who just bought pretzels and juice. I guess she really did have a lucky dime."

"And look at that stuffed animal she won, a teddy bear," Donna said. "Just what I want."

"Why don't we try the Dime Toss?" Diane asked.

13

"It's almost impossible to win," Eric told his sister. "That's what Freddy, the boy running the booth, told us. That's why he's giving away such good prizes."

"Look," Cam said. She pointed to the schoolyard gate. Cam said, *"Click,"* and closed her eyes. She said, *"Click,"* again.

"What are you pointing at?" Eric asked.

"Someone just rode out on a bicycle. It's the same bicycle we saw before, the one that wasn't locked."

Chapter Three

"Stop!" Cam yelled as she ran toward the gate. "Get off that bicycle!"

Eric and the twins followed Cam. They ran past the Baseball Throw and the refreshment stand. As they passed the Water Gun Shoot, one of the children missed the candle and hit Eric's ear.

At the gate, Cam waved her arms and yelled, "Stop!" But the girl on the bicycle didn't even turn around. She kept right on riding.

"What do we do now?" Eric asked as he wiped the water off his ear.

"I want to see where she's going."

While Cam and Eric stood by the gate, a few children came into the schoolyard. And a few left. The girl who had just won the Dime Toss was talking to a tall boy with curly blond hair.

"I can't see her anymore," Cam said. "Let's tell Ms. Benson what happened. She'll know what to do."

Cam, Eric, Donna, and Diane ran to Ms. Benson. They told her about the unlocked bicycle.

"We yelled to the girl and told her to stop," Cam said. "But she didn't. She just kept on riding."

"Maybe she didn't hear you."

"She heard us, all right," Eric told Ms. Benson. "Cam yelled really loud."

"Did you see who the girl was?"

"No. I only saw her from the back. She

was wearing a green sweater and she has long black hair."

"Can you describe the bicycle?"

Cam said, *"Click,"* and closed her eyes. "It was a girl's bike. It was red with some blue stripes and two baskets in the back."

Ms. Benson blew her whistle. She waited until it was quiet. Then she blew the whistle a second time and called out, "If anyone left a red-and-blue bicycle unlocked in the schoolyard, please come and see me."

The schoolyard became noisy again. The fifth-graders running the booths called out for children to try their luck. Cam and Eric waited with Ms. Benson. But no one came to tell them that a bicycle was missing.

"Maybe the bicycle wasn't stolen," Ms. Benson said.

"No, I'm sure it was stolen. That's why the girl didn't stop when I called to her," Cam said.

"Well, you don't have to wait here," Ms.

Benson said. "I'll call you if anyone comes for the bicycle."

"Then let's try the Button Jar Guess," Donna said. "The prize for the closest guess is a really big stuffed animal. It's a kangaroo mother with a baby in her pouch."

Cam, Eric, and the twins walked to the Button Jar Guess. There was a line of children waiting to guess the number of buttons in the jar. Before Cam got in line, she walked very close to the jar, said, *"Click,"* and blinked her eyes. Once Cam was in line, she said, *"Click,"* again and closed her eyes. Then she started counting.

"One, two, three . . ."

"What's she doing?" Diane whispered.

"She's looking at the picture of the jar she has in her head," Eric explained. "She's counting the buttons."

"Thirty-seven, thirty-eight, thirty-nine . . ."

"It's my turn," Diane said. She gave the boy running the game a nickel. He gave her a card. Diane wrote her guess on the card.

"Sixty-two, sixty-three, sixty-four . . ."

Donna and Eric guessed next. Then it was Cam's turn. Her eyes were still closed.

"Ninety-four, ninety-five, ninety-six . . ."

"Let's go," the boy running the booth told Cam. "Your memory won't help you with this game. Most of the buttons are hidden in the middle of the jar."

Cam opened her eyes. "Counting the buttons that I could see will help me to guess." Cam wrote down a number on the card and gave it to the boy.

Bong! Bong!

Freddy, the boy at the Dime Toss, was hitting the bottom of a large pot with a wooden spoon. "We have another winner," he called out.

A tall boy with curly blond hair, who was wearing a red baseball cap, was standing near the booth. He was smiling and holding a large furry toy elephant.

"Let's try that game," Donna said.

"We can try it," Eric said. "But I don't think we'll win."

As Cam, Eric, and the twins walked toward the Dime Toss, a girl on a bicycle

20

rode past. Cam looked at her and said, *"Click."* Then she said, *"Click,"* again and closed her eyes.

"That's the bicycle," Cam said when she opened her eyes. "And that's the girl who stole it.

"Come on," Cam said as she ran after the bicycle. "Let's catch her."

Chapter Four

Cam, Eric, Donna, and Diane caught up to the girl when she stopped to put her bicycle in the rack.

"That's Debby Lane," Eric whispered. "She wouldn't steal a bicycle."

"Debby, is this your bicycle?" Cam asked. The girl didn't turn around. And she didn't answer.

"Is this your bicycle?" Cam asked again. This time she spoke louder.

The girl still didn't answer. She put her

bicycle in the rack. Then she turned and saw Cam, Eric, and the twins.

"Oh, hi," she said.

"Why didn't you answer me?" Cam asked. "When you left the schoolyard I called to you. And I just spoke to you again."

"Wait a minute. I can't hear you," Debby Lane said. She turned off a radio strapped

to her waist. Then she took off a tiny set of earphones.

"You shouldn't wear those when you ride your bicycle," Donna said.

"If a car honks, you won't hear it. And you won't hear police sirens," Eric told her. "You won't know to get out of the way."

"And you should lock your bicycle," Cam said as she and Eric walked away. "Some-one might steal it."

Bong! Bong!

"We have a winner here. We have an-other winner!" Freddy called out from the Dime Toss booth.

"Let's hurry," Donna said. "Freddy must be wrong. That Dime Toss must be easy. I want to get there before he runs out of prizes."

A crowd had gathered around the Dime Toss booth. Inside the booth, on the ground, was a large sheet of cardboard with several circles drawn on it. Children

24

were throwing dimes, trying to get them to land in the middle of a circle.

A girl with her hair arranged in long brown braids and wearing sunglasses walked away from the booth. She was holding a large toy poodle.

"She must be the winner," Diane said.

Cam and Eric watched as the other children threw dimes onto the cardboard. A few dimes touched the edges of a circle. But none landed completely inside a circle. Every few minutes Freddy used a broom and swept the dimes into a box at the edge of the cardboard.

"Why don't you try?" Donna asked.

"We're studying the game," Eric said.

A tall, skinny girl threw a dime onto the cardboard. The dime bounced up and landed on the ground.

A young girl sat on the ground. She dropped a dime onto the cardboard. The dime started to spin in the middle of a

circle. Everyone near the booth watched as the dime spun slower and slower. Then it stopped with only half of the dime inside the circle.

"Did you see that?" Eric whispered to Donna. "The girl didn't win because the dime wasn't completely in the circle."

An older boy came to the booth. He sat on the ground and gently tossed a dime. It slid to the circle in the center of the cardboard and stopped.

"He won," Eric said.

Freddy took a wooden spoon from his pocket and banged it on the bottom of a large pot. "We have another winner," he called out. Then Freddy asked the boy which stuffed animal he wanted.

"I'll take that one," the boy said. He pointed to a large furry brown teddy bear.

Cam looked at the boy. He was tall, with curly blond hair. He was wearing a large brown cowboy hat.

"I think I know what to do now," Eric said. "I'll just try to slide the dime into the middle of a circle."

Eric held a dime. He sat on the ground. Before he tossed his dime onto the cardboard, he turned to Donna and Diane and said, "I'm playing this game for you. If I win, you two can share the prize."

Chapter Five

Eric gently tossed the coin. It slid past three circles and stopped just at the edge of the cardboard.

"We didn't win," Donna said.

Cam reached into her pocket. She took out a dime and said, "Let me try."

Cam sat on the ground. She carefully tossed the dime up in the air so that it landed flat on the cardboard. It landed near one of the circles.

"I don't see how anyone can win this game," Cam said as she got up from the ground. "It's just about impossible to get a dime right inside a circle."

"Let's try something else," Donna said. "Maybe we can win a prize at another booth."

"I'll bet you can win at the Trivia booth," Eric said to Cam. "When you say your *'Clicks'* you can remember all kinds of things."

As Cam, Eric, and the twins were walking toward the Trivia booth, they passed Ms. Benson. Cam and Eric stopped to ask Ms. Benson if she needed their help.

"Please check the bicycles again," Ms. Benson told them. "Then walk through the schoolyard. See if any of the young children are crying. Make sure there are no problems at any of the booths."

At the bicycle racks, Cam and Eric pulled at all the locks. They were all closed. Even Debby Lane's bicycle was locked.

The boy at the Button Jar Guess needed

paper. "I'm doing great," he told Cam and Eric. "I already have one hundred and ninety-four guesses."

Eric got some paper from Ms. Benson. He took it to the boy.

One of the rings at the Ring Toss broke. Cam helped tape it.

Cam, Eric, and the twins went to the Trivia booth last. The girl there said that her only problem was that so few children wanted to come to her booth.

"We can help you with that," Donna said. "Cam wants to take your test."

The girl opened up a folder. She was about to ask Cam a question when Freddy banged on the large metal pot again.

"We have another winner," he called out.

Cam turned. She saw a girl holding a large stuffed animal, a giraffe. The girl was smiling. She had braces on her teeth and was wearing a green hat.

"I don't understand how people keep

winning. That Dime Toss is impossible," Eric said.

"Your first question," the girl at the booth said, "is *How fast can an elephant run?* And you don't have to give me the exact answer, but you have to be close."

Cam said, *"Click,"* and closed her eyes. "I saw a chart in the Kurt Daub museum,"

Cam said. "It listed the speeds of different animals. Now, let's see. The cheetah was the fastest animal on the list. It runs seventy miles an hour. That's about one hundred and fifteen kilometers. And the elephant runs twenty-five miles an hour. That's about forty kilometers."

"That's right," the girl said. "You win a school banner. Do you want to try for another prize?"

"Yes," Donna said.

"All right," the girl said, reading from her folder, "in what year did an astronaut first walk on the moon?"

Cam said, *"Click,"* and closed her eyes. "His name is Neil Armstrong," Cam said, with her eyes still closed. "He first stepped on the moon on July 20, 1969."

"That's right," the girl said. "You win a school T-shirt."

Bong! Bong! Freddy banged on the large metal pot again.

"Look," Eric said to Cam, "there's another winner at the Dime Toss."

Cam opened her eyes. She turned to look at the Dime Toss booth. A tall boy was walking away from the booth. He was wearing a blue woolen stocking hat. It covered most of his hair. The boy was carrying a large teddy bear.

"Would you like to try one more question?" the girl at the Trivia booth asked.

"That boy looks familiar," Cam said, still looking at the Dime Toss.

"She'll try another question," Donna told the girl at the Trivia booth.

"Maybe she doesn't want to," Diane said.

Cam closed her eyes. She said, *"Click."* She said, *"Click,"* again.

"If you get this one right," the girl at the Trivia booth said, "you win a school notebook."

Cam opened her eyes. "I don't have time to play any more games," she told the girl. Then she said to Eric, "We have to go to the Dime Toss booth. There's something strange going on there."

Chapter Six

Cam and Eric ran to the Dime Toss. The booth was surrounded by children who were taking turns throwing dimes onto the cardboard.

"Hey, Freddy," Cam called. "I want to talk to you."

"Not now. I'm busy."

Cam and Eric watched the children throw their dimes onto the cardboard. Not one even came close to winning. Then a girl wearing a red baseball cap gently tossed a coin onto the cardboard. It slid and then stopped inside the circle in the center of the cardboard.

"I win," the girl said, and she smiled. She had braces on her teeth. There were only two prizes left. "I'll take that one," the girl said. She pointed to a little toy monkey.

Freddy gave the stuffed animal to the girl. She walked off with it. Then Freddy picked up the metal pot. He reached into his pocket and took out the wooden spoon.

"Don't bang on the pot," Cam said.

"But why not? I have a winner," Freddy said.

"There's something odd about that middle circle. Both times I was here, a dime suddenly stopped inside it. Maybe there's some jelly or glue on it."

Freddy took his broom and swept the dimes into the box at the edge of the cardboard. The winning dime didn't move. Freddy pushed harder on the broom and swept it into the box with the other dimes.

Cam felt the top surface of the cardboard. She told Eric and Freddy that it was smooth.

"You know," Freddy said, "now that I think about it, it *was* odd. Every winning dime was inside the same middle circle."

Cam sat on the ground in front of the booth. Eric sat next to her.

Cam closed her eyes and said, *"Click."* She told Eric, "I'm looking at the children

who won at the Dime Toss."

"I remember the first girl who won," Eric said. "She was standing in front of Donna and Diane at the refreshment stand. She was the girl who said she had a lucky dime."

Cam said, *"Click,"* again. She said it a few more times. Then Cam opened her eyes.

"I was looking at the pictures I have in my head of all the winners. That girl with the lucky dime didn't win just once. She won four times. And she wore disguises. She wore her hair long. Then she wore it in braids. She wore sunglasses once. And she kept changing hats."

"How do you know she was the same girl?" Freddy asked.

Eric said, "Disguises like that can fool some people, but they can't fool Cam's mental camera."

"And every time that girl smiled, I saw the braces on her teeth," Cam added.

"Excuse me," a tall boy said. "You're in my way."

Cam and Eric moved. The boy sat on the ground. He reached into his pocket and took out a dime. The boy was wearing sunglasses and a dark blue rain hat.

The boy gently tossed the coin onto the cardboard. It slid and then stopped right inside the middle circle.

The boy took the last stuffed animal as his prize. As he walked away, Cam looked

straight at the boy and said, *"Click."*

Freddy swept the last few dimes into the box. Then he sat next to Cam and Eric. He was holding the box of dimes.

"Well, that's it," Freddy said. "My booth is closed. I've given away the last prize."

Cam wasn't listening. Her eyes were closed again. And she kept saying, *"Click."* Then Cam jumped up. She started to run toward the schoolyard gate. "Come on," she called to Eric. "We have to catch that boy."

Chapter Seven

"Wait, Cam, wait," Eric called as he ran.

Eric caught up with Cam at the gate. She was standing there looking in all directions.

"I lost him," Cam said. "I don't know which way he went."

"What did he do?" Eric asked.

"That was the fourth time he won at the Dime Toss. He wore a different disguise every time, but it was the same boy. And when we ran after Debby on that bicycle, we passed him and that girl. They were talking to each other. They're in this to-gether."

"So what?" Eric said as he turned and started to walk back into the schoolyard. "Wearing a disguise isn't a crime. And we can't chase after every kid who wins a prize."

"But Eric, they must have done something wrong. How else could they keep winning?"

Cam walked with Eric into the school-yard. As they walked, Cam closed her eyes and said, *"Click."*

"Watch where you're walking," a boy said to Cam. "You almost bumped into me."

"What are you doing?" Eric asked.

Cam's eyes were open now. "I think we should look at those dimes," she told Eric.

Cam and Eric went back to the Dime Toss booth. Freddy was no longer there. They found him near the refreshment stand. He had just given the box of dimes to Ms. Benson.

"May we look through those dimes?" Cam asked Ms. Benson.

Ms. Benson gave Cam the box.

"Look at this," Cam said as she took out a coin. "This explains why that boy and girl kept winning."

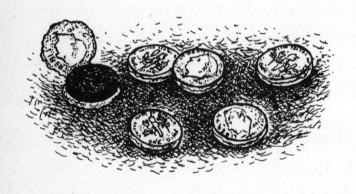

Freddy looked at the coin. Then Eric looked at it.

"It's shiny," Eric said. "And it's lumpy. But how did a lumpy dime help them win?"

"It's not a dime," Cam said as she looked

through the box. She took out a few more coins.

"Look," Cam said as she peeled the face off one of the coins. "They rubbed some aluminum foil over a real dime. Then they glued it to a round metal slug."

"But how did that help them win?" Freddy asked.

"Come on. I'll show you," Cam said. She gave the box of dimes to Ms. Benson. Cam kept the fake dimes and walked with Eric and Freddy to the Dime Toss booth.

Cam sat on the ground. Then she gently tossed one of the fake dimes onto the cardboard. It slid across the board and then stopped inside the center circle. Cam tossed another one. It did the same thing.

"What made this happen?" Freddy asked.

"I bet it was a magnet," Eric said.

Cam nodded and said, "When we first came to the carnival, we saw that boy leaving. He was carrying tape. You thought he was helping set up the carnival. He wasn't. I'll bet he taped a magnet right under the center circle."

Freddy lifted the cardboard. He found a magnet taped beneath it.

"That's why I always had trouble sweeping off the winning dimes," Freddy said. "But what do we do now?"

"We have to find those two. We can't let them keep all those prizes," Cam said. She started to run toward the gate.

Eric called to her. "Stop! We don't even know where to go. Let's find Ms. Benson. She'll tell us what to do."

Chapter Eight

Cam, Eric, and Freddy went to Ms. Benson. They told her everything that had happened at the Dime Toss booth.

"Once those children leave the schoolyard," Ms. Benson said, "there's very little I can do. I'll drive you to the police station. Maybe they can help."

They walked to Ms. Benson's car. It was a big old blue car. Books and papers were piled on the back seat. Eric began to open the back door.

"No, don't," Ms. Benson said.

It was too late. Books, papers, and a box wrapped in gift paper fell out. Eric and Freddy chased after the papers. They picked up the books and the gift. Then they climbed into the car. Cam sat in the front seat next to Ms. Benson.

"I think this will be the best fifth-grade carnival ever," Ms. Benson said as she drove. "All the prizes were donated, so all the money we make will go to the library. We may even have enough to buy a new encyclopedia."

"We made a whole boxful of dimes at my booth," Freddy said.

Ms. Benson waited at a traffic light. When the light turned green, she started to drive off.

"Don't go straight," Cam said. "Turn left."

"But that's not the way to the police station."

"I know. But I see something at the end of the block."

Ms. Benson put on her turn signal. As she made the turn, Eric said, "I see it, too."

A small table was set up. A tall boy with curly blond hair was calling out, "Bring home a toy for your children. Buy a soft, furry stuffed animal."

The girl with him had braces on her teeth and long brown hair. She was holding a toy giraffe. She was showing it to people who walked by.

"They won all those prizes at my Dime Toss," Freddy said.

"They didn't win," Eric said. "They cheated you out of them."

Ms. Benson parked her car. She told Cam, Eric, and Freddy to wait inside. She would talk to the two children.

As Ms. Benson walked from her car, the girl came over to her. She tried to sell Ms. Benson a teddy bear. Then Ms. Benson started to talk. She called to the tall boy.

"What's she saying?" Eric asked.

"I can't hear her," Cam said. "And I can't open the window. It's stuck."

"So is mine," Freddy said.

They watched as Ms. Benson talked to the two children. Then Ms. Benson walked back to the car. The two children followed her, carrying the stuffed animals.

"Jennifer, Eric, and Freddy," Ms. Benson said as she opened Cam's door, "I'd like you to meet Bert and Sylvia. They are going to give these prizes back. And they agreed to help in the library every Monday afternoon. Isn't that nice?"

Neither Bert nor Sylvia smiled. "Are you taking us to the police?" Bert asked.

Ms. Benson shook her head. "I'm sure you have learned your lesson," she said. Bert and Sylvia put the prizes into the trunk of Ms. Benson's car. Then they folded up the small table and walked off.

"Well, you children caught two thieves," Ms. Benson said as she drove back to school. "By cheating at the Dime Toss, they were stealing those prizes. You also solved a mystery. I was wondering why there were so many winners at Freddy's booth."

Later that afternoon, the winner of the Button Jar Guess was announced. A first-grade boy's guess was the closest. The toy kangaroo mother and baby that he won were almost as big as he was.

"I don't care if I didn't win," Donna said. "At least Cam won a school T-shirt for me."

"And she won a banner for me," Diane said.

Chapter Nine

A few days later, Cam and Eric were back in school. Spring vacation was over. At three o'clock, when the class was getting ready to go home, Ms. Benson asked Cam and Eric to wait. Then she walked with them to the library.

"Oh, there you are," the librarian said when they walked in. "Ms. Benson told me how you figured out what was happening at the Dime Toss. You two must read a lot of mysteries."

"We do," Eric said, "but that's not why

we can solve mysteries. It's Cam's memory. It's amazing. She remembers everything she sees."

The librarian told Cam and Eric that with the money from the fifth-grade carnival he bought a new encyclopedia. Inside the front cover of each volume he wrote, "This encyclopedia is a gift from the fifth grade."

Then the librarian took two mystery books off his desk and said, "Ms. Benson gave these books to the library. Look at what she wrote inside them."

Cam opened one of the books and read aloud, " 'These books were given to the school library in honor of two great solvers of mysteries, Jennifer Jansen and Eric Shelton.' "

When Cam and Eric left the library, Bert and Sylvia were busy working. Bert was putting books away on the shelves. Sylvia was sitting at a desk, fixing torn books with

tape. Bert and Sylvia pretended not to see Cam and Eric.

Cam and Eric had borrowed the two new mysteries. As they left school, Cam told Eric, "I don't think the mysteries in these books will be as easy to solve as the carnival mystery."

"Sure they'll be easy," Eric said. "We'll read carefully. We'll look for clues. And when you get near the end of the book, if you want to remember a clue from the beginning, you don't have to look back. Just close your eyes and say, *'Click'!*"